When the Frost Is on the Punkin

JAMES WHITCOMB RILEY

Illustrations by Glenna Lang

A Godine Storyteller

DAVID R. GODINE · PUBLISHER

BOSTON

For Esmé and her father Alex

First published in 1991 by

DAVID R. GODINE, PUBLISHER, INC.

Horticultural Hall

300 Massachusetts Avenue

Boston, Massachusetts 02115

First published in softcover in 1993

ISBN: 0-87923-912-3 (HC)

ISBN: 0-87923-988-3 (SC)

LC: 91-55368

First softcover printing, 1993

Printed in Hong Kong by South China Printing Company

When the Frost Is on the Punkin

When the frost is on the punkin
and the fodder's in the shock,

And you hear the kyouck and gobble
of the struttin' turkey-cock,
And the clackin' of the guineys,
and the cluckin' of the hens,

And the rooster's hallylooyer
as he tiptoes on the fence;

O it's then's the times a feller

is a-feelin' at his best,

With the risin' sun to greet him

from a night of peaceful rest,

As he leaves the house, bareheaded,
and goes out to feed the stock,
When the frost is on the punkin
and the fodder's in the shock.

They's something kindo' harty-like
about the atmusfere
When the heat of summer's over
and the coolin' fall is here—

QUEEN OF ALL SAINTS SCHOOL
1715 E. Barker Avenue
Michigan City, Indiana 46360

Of course we miss the flowers,
　　and the blossums on the trees,
And the mumble of the hummin'-birds
　　and buzzin' of the bees;

But the air's so appetizin';
  and the landscape through the haze
Of a crisp and sunny morning
  of the airly autumn days

Is a pictur' that no painter
    has the colorin' to mock—
When the frost is on the punkin
    and the fodder's in the shock.

The husky, rusty russel
    of the tossels of the corn,
And the raspin' of the tangled leaves,
    as golden as the morn;

The stubble in the furries—
    kindo' lonesome-like, but still
A-preachin' sermuns to us
    of the barns they growed to fill;

The strawstack in the medder,
and the reaper in the shed;

The hosses in theyr stalls below—
the clover overhead!—

O, it sets my hart a-clickin'
like the tickin' of a clock,
When the frost is on the punkin
and the fodder's in the shock!

James Whitcomb Riley was a great lover of local dialect. In *When the Frost Is on the Punkin*, many of the words he uses express the *real* sounds of things, like the "kyouck" sound of the turkey or the "hallylooyer" call of the rooster. Sometimes, he also uses a spelling closer to the way a word would sound when pronounced with a midwestern accent (Riley was from Indiana), such as "tossels" for "tassels," "airly" for "early," "furries" for "furrows," or "medder" for "meadow." Riley's dialect, his creative use of language, and the freedom of expression he adopted help make his poetry rich with the sounds, feelings, and rhythms of everyday life.

James Whitcomb Riley (1849–1916), known as "The Hoosier Poet," was the author of "Little Orphant Annie" and many other poems enjoyed by children. Making his start early in life playing the fiddle and reciting poetry to sell "Wizard Oil" in traveling medicine shows, he rose to great prominence in later life, with an honorary degree from Yale University and a day named in his honor.

Glenna Lang's illustrations have appeared frequently in *The Boston Globe*, *The Atlantic Monthly*, and other publications. Her past work includes illustrations for *My Shadow* by Robert Louis Stevenson (Godine), a children's Book-of-the-Month-Club alternate selection. She lives in Cambridge, Massachusetts, with her husband and daughter, Esmé.